By Yaa Dapaa

Taylor Tweet

To order additional copies of this book, contact:
Xlibris
1-888-795-4274
www.Xlibris.com
Orders@Xlibris.com

ISBN: Softcover   978-1-9845-8731-2
         EBook   978-1-9845-8730-5

Print information available on the last page

Rev. date: 07/31/2020

This Book Belongs To:

_____

One day at recess a boy named Kristen was making fun of Taylor's last name.

"Hey Taylor, why is your last name Tweet? Are you a bird?"

Taylor was sick of him always messing with her. First, he used to call her Faylor because she failed her test. Now, they were making fun of her last name. Before she knew it, all of the boys were making chirping sounds like a bird. Taylor felt like an erupting volcano. That's why this happened next.

Taylor pushed Kristen. At her school, Saint Washington, they had very strict rules about pushing and anything that would hurt someone. Taylor was in very serious trouble at school. Then she started wondering what her parents might do to punish her.

"They're probably just going to yell at me."

It was better than she thought, but only for a while. At first, her dad just yelled at her, but her evil stepmother convinced her dad to prohibit her from food, water, electronics, and going outside even for school! It hurt Taylor's dad to do it.

"Oh, and I forgot," said her evil stepmother, "You are never, ever going to have a single birthday party again!"

Tears started rolling down Taylor's cheeks. She was planning to make her tenth birthday a big party. But now, all she had to do was to forget it all. Taylor cried and cried.

"Cry me a river!" said her evil stepmother. "But I'll never change my mind!"

Taylor's stepmother seemed to be having an enjoyable time torturing Taylor. Taylor had a plan to run back to her real mom, Teagan Tweet, a famous singer who was secretly the queen Of the island of hope ..

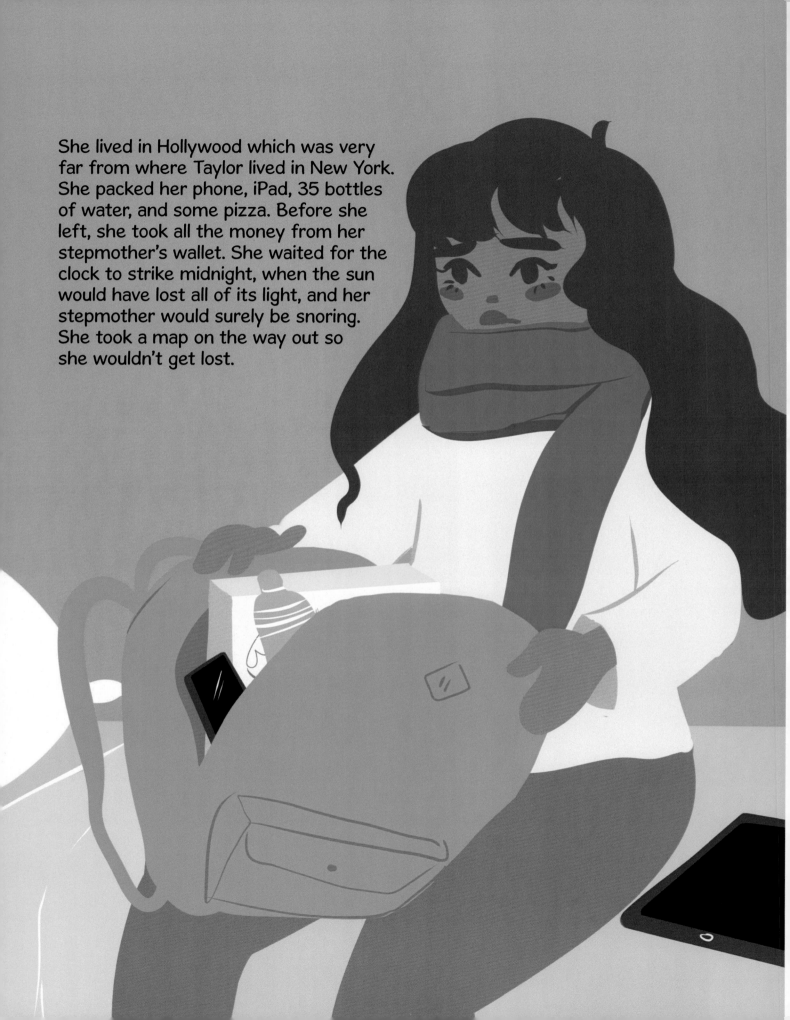

She lived in Hollywood which was very far from where Taylor lived in New York. She packed her phone, iPad, 35 bottles of water, and some pizza. Before she left, she took all the money from her stepmother's wallet. She waited for the clock to strike midnight, when the sun would have lost all of its light, and her stepmother would surely be snoring. She took a map on the way out so she wouldn't get lost.

That night it was really windy. Taylor could barely keep her eyes open. All of a sudden, the map flew out of Taylor's hands. She'd ran the fastest she ever ran in her life but she couldn't keep up with it. Taylor stood there watching it disappear right before her eyes.

Taylor felt like giving up, but she couldn't. She had a magical feeling inside her that made her keep walking. Taylor knew something really, really magical was going to happen.

Taylor bumped her head on a skyscraper and fell to the ground. She woke up the next day at 10:00 p.m. She realized she had slept through most of the day. Taylor suddenly heard voices saying, "IS SHE AWAKE?"

"NO! SHE'S DEAD!"

"Don't worry, she's just sleeping."

Taylor opened her eyes to see a blue tiger with emerald green eyes, and a golden flying fox whose eyes were a mysterious blue.

The other animals' eyes were shimmery neon colors.

"I must have hit my head real hard!" thought Taylor.

She closed her eyes and opened them. This time she saw the animals' fur glowing, and they had wings! She realized she was in a glowing forest too!

"You guys can talk?!" said Taylor.

The blue tiger explained that she had the power to talk to animals. Taylor was confused and frightened.

"Well, I should get going, I have to head for my mom's house," said Taylor.

"Taylor," said the golden flying fox.. "You are an animal princess. Your great-great-great grandmother sent us here to help you get to your mother's animal castle."

"Castle? Oh. Okay, we better start heading to my mom's castle," said Taylor.

"Hop on," said the golden flying fox.

They started heading toward Taylor's mom's castle. Taylor was still confused about being an animal princess, so she asked them to explain during the flight.

"You're the Princess of all animals that have wings. That is why your name is Tweet," said the lightning-blue tiger.

"Then wouldn't I be the Princess of birds?" said Taylor.

"I said you are the Princess of all animals that have wings, and there are a lot of half-bird animals that people think of as mythical creatures."

"Oh, I get it now."

The animals were hungry, so they stopped at a floating island in the sky.

Taylor offered them some pizza, but they told her, "As an animal princess, you shouldn't eat meat."

"I'm a vegetarian, but one day my stepmom brought home some veggie pizza because she thought I hated veggies, but then she realized I was a vegetarian, and started making me eat meat."

"That's horrible," said the flying fox.

"Well, at least I'm not going to see her again," said Taylor.

The animals used their powers to change the boxes of pepperoni pizza into power berries. Taylor loved the power berries. Taylor seemed to be gaining more power with each portion she ate.

They drank some water and then took off..They got to Teagan Tweet's house at 8:00 a.m.

Taylor's mom woke her up. She woke up and saw her real mom for the first time. Taylor hugged her mom very, very tight. It was the first time she had ever been happy in her life.

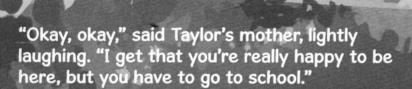

"Okay, okay," said Taylor's mother, lightly laughing. "I get that you're really happy to be here, but you have to go to school."

"School?" said Taylor.

"Yeah, school."

"But people are gonna make fun of me!"

"No, not anymore," said Taylor's mom.

Taylor got to wear whatever she wanted to her new school, Saint Mary. She found a rainbow skirt with a matching shirt. She wore it. In all her classes there were these kids named Wendy Woof, Morgan Moo, Olive Oink, and Asai Arf. They became her best friends. She loved her new school. She invited all her new friends to her tenth birthday. Her mom said she was going to surprise her.

TAYLOR ♡
HAPPY B-DAY

5 DAYS LATER

It was Taylor's tenth birthday . She was so excited that she couldn't think right. She didn't know what to wear. At lunchtime, Taylor was going to ask her mom to help pick out her outfit when she surprised Taylor with the most beautiful dress. It was Taylor's favorite color, teal. She loved it so much!

She quickly changed into it, and they got into a limousine. The limousine flew up to an island with a castle on it. As they got closer, Taylor started to realize that there were decorations on the island.

When they arrived, Taylor's mom blindfolded her. When she took the blindfold off, she saw all her friends and all the animals that helped her find her way.

"HAPPY BIRTHDAY, PRINCESS TAYLOR!!!!" they all said.

Taylor got to sit in a flower throne and was crowned. She and her friends flew high, high up.

When she looked down, Taylor could
see all of her old friends and all the
people who had been mean to her.
And for the first time, Taylor felt like
she had control.

The End

Printed in the United States
By Bookmasters